3-

GREAT ILLUSTRATED CLASSICS

REBECCA OF SUNNYBROOK FARM

Kate Douglas Wiggin

adapted by
Eliza Gatewood Warren

Illustrations by
Ed Tadiello

BARONET
B·O·O·K·S

BARONET BOOKS, New York, New York

GREAT ILLUSTRATED CLASSICS

edited by
Joshua E. Hanft

Contents

CHAPTER   PAGE

1. The Long Journey to Riverboro 7
2. An Icy Welcome 23
3. A Triumph in School.................... 37
4. The Breaking Storm 51
5. The Miracle of the Rainbow 65
6. Rebecca Rallies to a Good Cause 81
7. Two Remarkable People Meet 99
8. Thanksgiving Surprises 115
9. A Christmas to Remember 133
10. Challenging Times 151
11. An Understanding Heart............... 169
12. A Heavy Load for Young Shoulders 187
13. A Bittersweet Graduation 205
14. The Dawning of a New Day 225

About the Author

Kate Douglas Wiggin was born Kate Smith in Philadelphia on September 28, 1856 and lived in that city until the age of three when her father died. It was then that young Kate and her mother moved to Hollis, Maine.

Growing up, Kate's main interest in life was books and one of her favorite authors was the English novelist, Charles Dickens, who she met once. Kate was educated at various schools in New England including Abbot Academy in Andover, Massachusetts.

At seventeen, Kate moved with her family to Santa Barbara, California, where she wrote her first short story, "Half a Dozen Housekeepers". It was published serially in *St. Nicholas Magazine* in 1897.

She went to San Francisco soon after, organized the first free kindergarten west of the

Rocky Mountains, and married Samuel Wiggin, a lawyer. Her first book, *The Story of Patsy*, was followed by *The Birds' Christmas Carol*, an enormously popular children's book.

More stories about children, which formed the bulk of Mrs. Wiggin's writing, followed, including the Penelope books, the adventures of an American girl and her friends in England where the author vacationed frequently.

Mrs. Wiggin's health was frail, and she spent a great deal of time in sanatoriums. During one such enforced rest, she wrote *Rebecca of Sunnybrook Farm*. Rebecca and her subsequent adventures in magazine serials, on the stage, and in motion pictures brought Mrs. Wiggin international fame.

The author died alone at a convalescent home in England in August, 1923, soon after completing her excellent biography, *My Garden of Memory*. Her ashes were scattered on the waters of the Saco River in Maine.

The Mail and One Passenger

Chapter One

The Long Journey to Riverboro

One warm day in May, Jeremiah Cobb was driving the stagecoach along the dusty road from Maplewood to Riverboro. Lolling back in his seat atop the coach, he held the horses' reins loosely in his hands and chewed his wad of tobacco.

Mr. Cobb carried the mail and one passenger—a small dark-haired girl about ten or eleven named Rebecca Randall. She was so thin and her brown calico dress so stiffly starched that she kept sliding back and forth on her leather seat. Whenever the wheels of the coach hit a rut, she bounced up and down in the air. It was all she could do just to keep her straw bonnet on straight.

Her mother had put her on the stagecoach in Maplewood a half hour earlier along with her trunk, a pink parasol, and a large bunch of lilacs.

"I want you to take Rebecca to my sisters in Riverboro," Mrs. Randall told Mr. Cobb. "Do you know Miranda and Jane Sawyer? They live in the brick house."

"Bless my soul. I know them well," Mr. Cobb assured her.

"Well, Rebecca is going there. They're expecting her. Will you keep on eye on her, please?" Mrs. Randall asked. "Good-bye, Rebecca. Try not to get into any mischief. Sit still, so you'll look nice and neat when you arrive."

"Good-bye," said Rebecca, giving her mother a hug and a kiss. "Don't worry. It's not like I haven't traveled before."

"Miranda will have her hands full, I guess,"

"They Live in the Brick House."

Aurelia Randall muttered to herself, as she watched the stagecoach disappear from view. "I wonder if living with her and Jane won't be the making of Rebecca."

After the stagecoach had rumbled along the winding country road several miles, Mr. Cobb heard a small voice call from the cabin below. He looked over his shoulder and saw Rebecca hanging out the window. Her hat had fallen down behind her head, and her one long dark braid was blowing in the breeze.

"Does it cost any more to ride up there with you?" she cried, waving her parasol at him. "I'm just rattling around down here. I'll be black and blue by the time we get to River-boro."

"You can come up here if you want to," Mr. Cobb shouted back. "There ain't no **extry** charge to sit with me." Then he stopped the coach, helped Rebecca out and up to the dri-ver's seat, and resumed the journey.

Smiling broadly, Rebecca sat down beside

Rebecca Hanging Out the Window

Mr. Cobb. She smoothed her dress under her carefully and shoved her bonnet back in place. "Oh, this is better!" she exclaimed. "I am a real passenger now. I hope we have a long long way to go."

"We have about two more hours," Mr. Cobb responded, good-naturedly. "It's a hot day. Why don't you put up your parasol?"

"Oh, dear, no! I never put it up when the sun shines. Pink fades quickly, you know," Rebecca said, covering her precious parasol with her dress. "Did you notice that the handle is scarred? That's because Fanny chewed it in church when I wasn't looking."

"Is Fanny your sister?" asked Mr. Cobb.

"She's one of them," Rebecca explained. "There are seven of us in all. Hannah is the oldest. I come next, then John, then Jenny, then Mark, then Fanny, then Mira, who was born the day Father died. She's three now."

"Well, I'll be. That is a big family!" Mr. Cobb said, inserting more tobacco in his left

"There Are Seven of Us."

cheek.

"Hannah and I have been taking care of babies for years," Rebecca told Mr. Cobb. "Aunt Miranda actually wanted Hannah instead of me, but Mother couldn't spare her. Hannah is better at housework than I am, you see. Mother has her hands full just running the farm."

"Oh, you live on a farm, do you?" Mr. Cobb asked. "Where is it?—near to where you got on?"

"Near? Oh, no, it must be thousands of miles away," Rebecca said. "The nearest town is Temperance. That's where we went to catch the train to Maplewood. We arrived there yesterday and spent the night at Cousin Ann's house. Then she drove us to Maplewood this morning to the stage stop."

"Does your farm have a name?" Mr. Cobb inquired.

"Mother calls it Randall's Farm, but I call it Sunnybrook Farm," Rebecca announced proudly. "Can you guess why?"

"I Call It Sunnybrook Farm."

"I suppose there's a brook somewhere near it," the old-timer said cautiously.

"That's a pretty good guess," Rebecca told him. "There's a brook, but it's not an ordinary brook. It's a very special brook that has a sandy bottom with lots of shiny pebbles. Whenever the sun shines, the brook catches its rays and sparkles—sometimes all day long. Does your stomach feel hollow? Mine does. I was so afraid I'd miss the stage I couldn't eat any breakfast."

"You better eat your lunch then. I won't eat until I get on down to Milltown."

"I hope I get to see Milltown someday," Rebecca said, unwrapping her lunch and taking a bite of her buttered corn muffin. "I suppose it's the grandest town in all Maine."

"If your Aunt Mirandy will let you, I'll drive you there someday soon when the stage ain't full," Mr. Cobb offered.

A thrill of delicious excitement ran through Rebecca. "Oh, that would be wonderful!" she

A Bite of Her Buttered Muffin

exclaimed.

"There's the river over there," Mr. Cobb pointed out. "This is the last long hill. When we get to the top of it, we'll see the chimneys of Riverboro. It ain't far now."

Suddenly, Rebecca stiffened in her seat. "I didn't think I was going to be nervous about coming to live with Aunt Miranda and Aunt Jane, but I guess I am," she admitted.

"Would you go back?" asked Mr. Cobb curiously.

"I'd never go back," Rebecca said with great dignity. "I might be scared, but I'd be ashamed to run. Going to Aunt Miranda's is like going down in the cellar in the dark. There might be ogres and giants, but then, there might be elves and fairies and enchanted frogs."

"Would you like to make a grand entrance?" Mr. Cobb asked. "I'll drive fast, and you hold your lilacs in your lap and open your parasol. We'll make the natives sit up and take notice."

"I don't think we better do that," Rebecca

"We'll See the Chimneys."

said. "Mother put me inside, and maybe she'd want me to be there when I arrive. Would you stop a minute and let me change places?"

"We've had a great trip, haven't we?" said Mr. Cobb, as he helped Rebecca back in the coach. In their short time together, he had really grown to like her and to admire her spirit and her courage. "You won't forget about Milltown?"

"Never," Rebecca promised. "Cross my heart."

Mr. Cobb climbed back up to his perch, and the stage clattered down the main street of Riverboro.

Rebecca sat quietly in her seat, clutching her bouquet of lilacs and her pink parasol. Beneath her calico dress, her heart beat wildly. Tears swam in her eyes. Her long journey had ended, and her new life with her two spinster aunts was about to begin.

The Main Street of Riverboro

For the Twentieth Time

Chapter Two

An Icy Welcome

"The stage ought to be here by now," said Miranda Sawyer, glaring nervously at the tall clock in the hall for the twentieth time. "I certainly thought that Aurelia would have sent us the child we asked for. It's just like her to palm off that wild one on us."

"Rebecca was just a tiny little thing when we saw her three years ago," ventured Miranda's sister, Jane. "She's had time to improve."

"And time to grow worse," Miranda snorted.

"Won't it be a privilege to put her on the right track?" asked Jane timidly, peeking out

23

the window for a glimpse of the stagecoach.

"I don't know about the privilege part. It'll be a considerable chore, I guess," Miranda snapped. "If her mother hasn't got her on the right track by now, it's probably too late."

"Look, Miranda, here they come now," cried Jane, rushing to the side door. She and her sister hurried outside and waited anxiously by the hollyhocks.

The dusty stagecoach rumbled up to the side entrance of the Sawyers' brick house, and Mr. Cobb helped Rebecca out like a real lady passenger.

"Hello, Aunt Jane. Hello, Aunt Miranda," Rebecca said eagerly, stepping forward to present her aunts with her bouquet of lilacs.

"You needn't have bothered to bring flowers," Miranda said, giving her niece a peck on the cheek. "The garden is always full of them."

Ignoring her sister, Jane stepped up and hugged Rebecca warmly. "Put the trunk in the hall, Jeremiah," she said. "We'll get someone

Like a Real Lady

to carry it upstairs later. You shouldn't leave your horses for long."

"Well, good-bye, Rebecca. Good-bye, ladies," Mr. Cobb said, depositing the trunk by a hall table and backing out the door. "You've got a lively little girl there."

"We're not much used to noise," Miranda remarked acidly, as she shut the door in Mr. Cobb's face. The poor man departed, wishing he had used any word other than lively.

"I'll take you upstairs and show you your room," Miranda told her niece. "Rub your feet on that braided rug you see there. Hang your bonnet and sunshade in the entry when you go past."

"May I keep my parasol in my room, Aunt Miranda? I think it might be safer there."

"There aren't any thieves about, and if there were, I guess they wouldn't want your sunshade. But come along," her aunt retorted. "Remember to always go up the back way. We don't use the front stairs on account of the car-

"We're Not Much Used to Noise."

pet."

Miranda led her niece up the back stairs and down the hall to her new bedroom. She opened the door for Rebecca, showed the child inside, and then mysteriously, she disappeared.

Rebecca stood perfectly still in the middle of the floor and looked about her. There was a square of oilcloth in front of each piece of furniture and a braided rug beside the four poster bed, which was covered with a fringed white dimity bedspread. A long, narrow window overlooked the back buildings and the barn.

Despite the fact it was a nice room, and much more comfortable than her room at home, Rebecca suddenly felt uneasy. Overwhelmed by feelings of anxiety, which she didn't completely understand, she tossed her umbrella in a corner and ripped off her bonnet. Then she yanked the bedspread down, jumped into the bed, and pulled the spread over her head.

A moment later, the door opened and Mi-

Rebecca Stood Perfectly Still.

randa walked right in without knocking. "Rebecca!" she shouted at the top of her lungs, "what are you doing in bed in the daytime dirtying the linens with your dusty boots?"

"I'm sorry, Aunt Miranda," Rebecca murmured apologetically. "Something came over me. I don't know what."

"Well, if it comes over you again very soon, we'll have to find out what it is," Miranda quipped. "Spread your bed up this minute, young lady. Our neighbor, Abijah Flagg, is bringing your trunk upstairs. I wouldn't want him to see such a messy room for anything. He'd tell it all over town."

Rebecca got right up and made her bed neatly. After Miranda and Abijah Flagg left, she unpacked her trunk herself and put all her clothes away in the wardrobe and chest of drawers. Then she combed and rebraided her hair, so she would be ready for supper.

However, she did so with a heavy heart. The truth was that she didn't feel welcome here

"What Are You Doing?"

and missed her warm, loving family at Sunnybrook Farm.

Rebecca arrived in Riverboro on a Friday. On Sunday afternoon after church, she sat down at the pine desk in her room and wrote her first letters home.

Dear Mother,

I am safely here. My dress was not wrinkled much, and Aunt Jane helped me press it. The brick house looks just the same as you told us. The parlor is beautiful and gives me creeps and chills when I look in the door. The furniture is elegant, too, but there are no good places to sit except in the kitchen. The same cat is here, but they do not save kittens when she has them, and the cat is too old to play with. Hannah told me once that you ran away with Father. If Aunt Miranda would run away, I should like to live with Aunt Jane. She seems to like me, but Aunt Miranda hates me. Everything I do irritates her. I wish Hannah had

Her First Letters Home

come instead of me, for it was Hannah they wanted. She is better behaved than I am and does not answer back so quickly. I miss you.

Your affectionate daughter,
Rebecca

Dear John,

Do you remember when we tied the new dog in the barn, and he bit the rope and howled? I am just like him. Only the brick house is the barn, and I cannot bite Aunt Miranda because I must be grateful for the opportunity she is giving me. My education is going to be the making of me and help us pay off the mortgage on the farm when we grow up.

I start school tomorrow. I am excited but scared, too. Say a little prayer for me.

Your loving sister,
Rebecca

"I Cannot Bite Aunt Miranda . . ."

The Schoolhouse Stood on a Crest.

Chapter Three

A Triumph In School

Bright and early Monday morning, Miranda drove Rebecca to school in Riverboro Center in a horse and wagon she borrowed from a neighbor.

The little schoolhouse, with its flagpole on top and its two doors in front, one for boys and the other for girls, stood on the crest of a hill. There were rolling fields and meadows on one side and a stretch of pine woods on the the other. In the distance, the Pleasant River sparkled in the morning sunlight.

Miranda led Rebecca inside the schoolhouse

and introduced her to the teacher, Miss Dearborn, who gave her new student a stack of books and ushered her to her seat.

From the beginning, school was the bright spot in Rebecca's life. She loved her studies and enjoyed her classmates immensely—particularly Emma Jane Perkins, who lived near her. The two girls walked to school together almost every day. Sometimes they were joined by the Simpson children, a large unruly brood, whose clothes were always patched and darned. They reminded Rebecca of her own big family.

Miss Dearborn had so much trouble deciding what grade to put Rebecca in, that after two weeks, she finally gave up. Rebecca joined Dick Carter and Living Perkins's reading group, studied arithmetic with lisping little Thuthan Thompson, explored geography with Emma Jane, and learned history with Alice Robinson. After school, she agonized over grammar with Miss Dearborn.

Miss Dearborn Gave Her a Stack of Books.

Despite her struggle with spelling and punctuation, Rebecca loved to write poetry and sent many of her best poems home to her mother and her brother, John, who kept them in a box with his birds' eggs.

Every Friday afternoon, the students at Riverboro Center School gave a recital of songs, poems, and speeches for an audience of parents and younger brothers and sisters. But the students hated this event, and Miss Dearborn always went home with a throbbing headache.

However, an amazing thing happened when Rebecca arrived on the scene. She loved these Friday recitals and participated so wholeheartedly that her enthusiasm was catching. Soon her classmates were reciting their pieces with zeal and were really enjoying themselves. Miss Dearborn was so pleased that she invited a group of community leaders to attend a special Friday afternoon performance.

On the morning of the recital, Living

She Loved These Recitals.

Perkins, a budding artist, decorated one of the blackboards with a map of North America. On the other blackboard, Rebecca, who was equally talented, drew the American flag with a figure of Columbia, copied from the top of a cigar box.

Miss Dearborn was delighted. "Let's give Rebecca a big hand for drawing such a beautiful picture," she exclaimed, standing back and admiring her student's artwork. "This is something the whole school can be proud of."

"Living and Rebecca should sign their pictures, so all our visitors will know who drew them," Dick Carter called from the back of the room.

As her classmates clapped and cheered in approval, Rebecca's heart leaped for joy. She had spent her young life working hard and had never before received such praise. It was a moment of great triumph.

Miss Dearborn dismissed the morning session early, so that the children who lived near-

Rebecca Drew the American Flag.

by could go home to change their clothes for the recital. Emma Jane and Rebecca ran nearly every step of the way.

Rebecca found the side door to the brick house locked, but she knew the key was under the steps. She unlocked the door and went in the dining room to find her lunch on the table. There was a note from Aunt Jane saying they had gone to Moderation with Mrs. Robinson.

Rebecca gulped down a piece of bread and butter and flew up the front stairs to her bedroom. On the bed lay the pink gingham dress Aunt Jane had just finished making that morning.

"Do I dare wear it without asking?" Rebecca wondered. "I don't see why Aunt Miranda and Aunt Jane would mind. After all, it's only gingham."

Hurriedly, Rebecca put on the pretty pink gingham dress, unbraided her pigtails, combed out her hair, and tied it back with a ribbon. Just for fun, she picked up her cher-

The Key Was Under the Steps.

ished pink parasol to show all the girls at school. On the way out, she noticed that the clock in the front hall said twenty minutes to one. She would have to hurry to get back to school on time.

"Rebecca Randall!" exclaimed Emma Jane, as the two girls met at the entrance to the school, "you're pretty as a picture! But how on earth did your Aunt Mirandy let you wear that brand-new dress?"

"They were both away, and I couldn't ask," Rebecca explained, walking up the front steps. "Why? Do you think they'd have said no?"

"Miss Mirandy always says no, doesn't she?" said Emma Jane.

"Yes," Rebecca agreed, as she opened the front door of the school for her friend, "but this is a very special occasion."

Rebecca had never been more right in her life. The afternoon was simply one triumph after another for the performers. The parents were proud as peacocks, and Miss Dearborn

"You're Pretty as a Picture!"

received many complimentary remarks about her teaching ability.

However, she couldn't help but wonder if some of the credit shouldn't go to Rebecca who was a natural leader and inspired her classmates to do their best. The bright-eyed girl stood in the center of the stage, and her voice soared above all the rest in the chorus. All eyes were upon her, and the crowd clapped wildly when the recital came to an end.

Afterward, Rebecca walked home happy and proud. Thick clouds were gathering in the sky, but the excited child never noticed. When she entered the side yard of the brick house, she saw Miranda standing in the open doorway, her hands on her hips and a scowl on her face. Poor Rebecca's heart sank. Instinctively, she knew there was trouble ahead.

The Crowd Clapped Wildly.

Miranda Shouted at Her Niece.

Chapter Four

The Breaking Storm

"Rebecca, come inside this minute," Miranda shouted at her niece, who stood forlornly at the bottom of the front stairs. "Would you please tell me why you wore that brand-new gingham dress to school without asking permission?"

"I had intended to ask you at noon, but you weren't at home, so I couldn't," Rebecca began, as she crept up the stairs and slipped in the front door. Out of the corner of her eye, she saw Aunt Jane dash, quick as a flash, into the kitchen.

"I don't believe a word you're saying," Miranda replied, putting her hands on her hips and blocking Rebecca's path. "You put that dress on because you were left alone. You knew perfectly well I wouldn't let you wear it."

Looking her aunt squarely in the eye, Rebecca said, "If I'd been certain that you wouldn't have let me, I'd never have worn the dress. I thought you wouldn't mind because we were having a real exhibition at school."

"Exhibition!" exclaimed Miranda scornfully. "The only exhibition was you showing off with that pink parasol of yours. Why, you were strutting home with all the airs and graces of your fancy, useless father."

Suddenly, Rebecca felt herself grow hot and flushed with anger. "Look here, Aunt Miranda," she cried, as she moved around behind her aunt and edged slowly toward the back stairs. "I'll be as good as I know how to be as long as I live here, but I won't allow you to call my father names. He was a wonderful father and a

"I Don't Believe a Word."

good music and dance instructor. It's mean of you to insult him."

"Don't you dare talk to me in that tone of voice, Rebecca Randall," Miranda barked, red in the face now. "Your father was a vain, foolish, shiftless man, and you might as well hear it from me as anybody else. He spent your mother's money and left her with seven children to provide for."

"It's pretty remarkable to leave seven nice children," sobbed Rebecca, with tears streaming down her face.

"Not when other folks have to help feed, clothe, and educate them," responded Miranda haughtily. "Not when they're as crafty and underhanded as you. Why, you used the front stairs at noon today. I know because you dropped your handkerchief. You left the screen in your bedroom window open, and now the house is full of flies. And what's more, you left the side door open till three o'clock, so anybody could have come in and stolen what they liked.

"Seven Nice Children"

Now, what do you have to say for yourself?"

"I'm sorry, Aunt Miranda," Rebecca said, sobbing all the harder. "I was just in a terrible hurry today. I had to get back to school in time for the recital. I'm really sorry."

"Excuses! Excuses!" Miranda fairly shouted, shaking her finger at Rebecca. "Now you go to bed. There's a bowl of milk and crackers on your bureau. I don't want to hear a word from you till morning. And you, Jane, out there in the kitchen. You go outside and take the dish towels off the line and close the shed doors. We're going to have a terrible storm."

"We've already had it," said Jane quietly from the kitchen door after Rebecca had left. "I don't often speak my mind, Miranda, but you shouldn't have made those unkind remarks about Lorenzo. He was what he was, and that can't be changed, but he was Rebecca's father. Aurelia always said he was a good husband."

"Yes, I've noticed that dead husbands are

"We've Already Had It," Said Jane.

usually good ones," Miranda replied sarcastically. "I tell you that child won't amount to a hill of beans till she gets her father trounced out of her. I'm glad I said what I did."

"I dare say you are," Jane spoke up bravely. "But it wasn't good manners, and it wasn't good religion, so don't expect me to approve." With these parting words, she rushed outside to do her chores before the storm broke.

A clap of thunder shook the house, as Rebecca, weary and down-hearted, climbed the back stairs to the second floor. She closed the door of her bedroom, took off the pink gingham dress with trembling hands, and put her good shoes away in the wardrobe.

For a long while, she sat by the window and watched the lightning play over the hilltop and the streams of rain chase each other down the lightning rod. Oh, how the storm outside echoed her own inner turmoil!

"You would think Aunt Miranda would be pleased that the niece she had invited down

She Watched the Lightning Over the Hilltop.

from the farm had done so well in school," Rebecca thought to herself, brushing away the tears. "Unfortunately, there's no hope of pleasing her. The best thing I can do is to go home and let Mother send Hannah to Riverboro in my place."

With this plan in mind, Rebecca jumped up and put on her oldest dress and shoes. "I'll go to Maplewood on the stage tomorrow with Mr. Cobb. Somehow I'll get home from Cousin Ann's," she plotted. "Oh, dear, Aunt Miranda and Aunt Jane aren't going to like this. Well, I'll just have to run away—that's all."

Hurriedly, Rebecca wrapped some clothes in a bundle and dropped it out the window. She could hear the sound of the sewing machine in the dining room and the chopping of meat in the kitchen, so she knew where both aunts were.

Without a backward glance, the determined girl scrambled out the window. Catching hold of the lightning rod, she stepped down onto a

She Put on Her Oldest Dress and Shoes.

cleat that had been left there by a workman, and inched her way gingerly to the woodbine trellis, which served as the perfect ladder. When she reached the bottom rung, she jumped down onto the porch and scooped up her bundle of clothes that had landed in the bushes nearby.

With the storm raging around her, Rebecca ran as fast as her legs would carry her down the muddy road that led out of Riverboro.

She Reached the Bottom Rung.

"Please May I Come In?"

Chapter Five

The Miracle of the Rainbow

Jeremiah Cobb was eating supper alone in his kitchen the afternoon of the storm since "Mother", as he called his wife, was visiting a sick neighbor. He had just gulped down the last bite of stew when he heard a loud knock at the door.

"Please may I come in, Mr. Cobb?" asked the poor drenched child who stood shivering on the front steps. The rain still fell in torrents, and the sky was dark even though it was only five o'clock.

"Well, I declare! It's my favorite passenger,"

said Mr. Cobb, who almost didn't recognize Rebecca because of her red eyes and swollen face. Never had he seen anyone look so sad and miserable. "Come to call on old Uncle Jerry and pass the time of day, have ye? Come in and warm yourself by the kitchen stove."

A compassionate man, Mr. Cobb felt his heart go out to Rebecca in her distress. His first thought was to do everything in his power to help her.

Immediately, he escorted her into the kitchen and hung her wet jacket on a nail to dry. As his visitor stood warming her hands by the stove, he took a seat at the table.

Unable to contain herself a moment longer, Rebecca cried, "Oh, Mr. Cobb, I've run away from the brick house and want to go back to the farm. Will you let me stay overnight and take me to Maplewood on the stage tomorrow? I haven't got any money for my fare, but I'll earn it somehow afterward."

"Well, I guess we won't quarrel about

"Come Warm Yourself by the Stove."

money," said the old man. "Now you come over here and tell me what's wrong."

Fighting the tears, Rebecca related the sad story of her problems with her Aunt Miranda. "You will take me to Maplewood on the stage, won't you?" she begged at the conclusion of her tale.

"I suppose your mother will be terribly glad to see you again?" asked Mr. Cobb, spreading some tomato preserves on a piece of bread for Rebecca. "Would you please pour me some tea?"

Obediently, Rebecca sat at the head of the table, munched on her snack, and poured a cup of tea for Mr. Cobb from a beautiful blue china teapot. "She won't like the fact I ran away, I suppose," Rebecca mused. "She'll be sorry I couldn't please Aunt Miranda, but I'll make her understand—just like I did you."

"I guess your mother was thinking about your schooling when she sent you here? But land! You can go to school in Temperance, can't

A Beautiful Blue China Teapot

you?" Mr. Cobb wanted to know.

"Unfortunately, that school is only open two months a year," Rebecca replied thoughtfully. "I can't go to any other schools because they are all too far away."

"Oh, well! There's other things in life beside education," responded Mr. Cobb, attacking a piece of apple pie with vigor.

"Yes, but Mother thought my education was going to be the making of me," returned Rebecca sadly, giving a little sob as she sipped a cup of tea.

"It'll be nice for all of you to be together again at the farm," Mr. Cobb commented, watching for Rebecca's reaction carefully. "Of course, it'll be a full house."

"It'll be too full. That's the trouble," Rebecca acknowledged. "But I'll make Hannah come to Riverboro in my place."

"Suppose Mirandy and Jane don't want her? I should be afraid they wouldn't," the clever old codger remarked. "They might be kinda

Attacking a Piece of Apple Pie

mad at you for running away, and you could hardly blame them."

"That hadn't occurred to me," Rebecca said quietly, stunned at the thought her sister might not be welcome at the brick house because of her sudden, unannounced departure.

"How's the school down here in Riverboro— pretty good?" inquired Jeremiah Cobb cagily.

"Oh, it's a splendid school," Rebecca admitted. "And Miss Dearborn is a wonderful teacher."

"She likes you, too," Mr. Cobb said. "Why, just the other day, she told Mother that you were her best student."

"Oh, did she really say that?" glowed Rebecca. "I've tried hard up to now, but I'll study the covers right off my books from here on."

"You mean you would if you were going to stay here," Mr. Cobb pointed out with raised eyebrows. "It's too bad you have to give up everything because of your Aunt Mirandy being so cranky. But I don't blame you. Now if

"That Hadn't Occurred to Me."

you'd asked my advice yesterday, I'd have re-minded you, that despite her faults, your aunt has seen to it you got new clothes, room and board, and some real fine schooling. Maybe you should have worked just a little harder to get along with her. And what about your Aunt Jane?"

"Oh, Aunt Jane and I get along beautifully. I like her better all the time."

"She'll be real sorry to find you gone tomor-row, I guess," the stagecoach driver interject-ed. "Why, only last week at prayer meeting she told Mother you had given her a new lease on life. Mother said she'd never seen Jane Sawyer look so young and happy."

There was a silence in the kitchen now. It was a silence that was broken only by the tick-ing of the tall clock and the beating of Rebec-ca's heart, which she thought almost drowned out the clock.

The rain had stopped, and through the win-dow a rainbow arch could be seen spanning

"You Should Have Worked a Little Harder."

the sky like a radiant bridge. "Bridges take one across difficult places," thought Rebecca. "Uncle Jerry seems to have built a bridge over my troubles and given me strength to walk in the right direction."

"The storm's over now," said the old-timer, filling his pipe. "We'll have sunny skies when you and I drive upriver tomorrow."

Rebecca pushed her teacup away, rose quietly from the table, and put on her jacket. "I'm not going with you, Mr. Cobb," she said with conviction. "I don't know if Aunt Miranda will want me after I've run away, but I'm going back while I have the courage. Will you go with me?"

"You better believe your Uncle Jerry won't leave till he gets things fixed up," cried Mr. Cobb with delight. "My plan is to drive you over to the brick house in my buggy. I will go to the side door and ask your aunts to step out to the shed to discuss a load of wood I'm delivering this week. Then you slip out of the

Like a Radiant Bridge

buggy and go upstairs to bed. The front door won't be locked, will it?"

"Not this time of night," Rebecca answered. "Aunt Miranda doesn't lock the door until she goes to bed, but oh, what if it should be?"

"Well, it won't," Mr. Cobb told the worried child. "If it is, we'll have to face it. In my opinion, no harm's been done. You ain't run away yet. You only came over to consult me about running away. We decided it ain't worth the trouble. Now come along with me. I'm all hitched up over at the post office."

"Oh, Mr. Cobb," Rebecca cried, picking up her bundle of clothes and following him out the door, "you've been a wonderful friend. You and the rainbow have helped me see things in a whole new light. Now I just hope and pray that your plan works. I have to admit that I'm nervous about this. What if something goes wrong, and my aunts catch me sneaking back in?"

"You Only Came to Consult."

It Worked Like a Charm.

Chapter Six

Rebecca Rallies to a Good Cause

Mr. Cobb's scheme to drive Rebecca home
and help her sneak back in the brick house un-
noticed by her aunts worked like a charm.
While the crafty coachman parked his buggy
in the side yard and lured Miranda and Jane
Sawyer out to the shed to discuss a delivery of
wood, Rebecca slipped silently in the front
door. Then she crept upstairs to her room and
undressed in the dark.

As she lay in bed mulling over the day's
events, she felt strangely at peace. She knew
that she had done the right thing to return to

the Sawyer homestead and was determined now to win Miranda's approval.

"I never saw a child improve in her work like Rebecca has," Miranda remarked to Jane a week later as they prepared dinner in the kitchen. "That settling down I gave her was probably just what she needed. I dare say it'll last for a month at least."

"I'm glad you're pleased," returned Jane, giving the bread dough she was kneading an extra thump. "A cringing worm is what you want, not a bright, smiling child. Rebecca looks to me as if she'd been through the Seven Years' War."

If her home life left much to be desired, school and the wonderful friendships Rebecca had helped make up for it. The bond Rebecca forged with Jeremiah Cobb, the wise, kind-hearted stagecoach driver who stood by her in her time of trouble, continued to grow.

True to his word, Mr. Cobb took Rebecca to Milltown on the stage for a day of sight-seeing

"Settling Down Was What She Needed."

in early October. Mrs. Cobb and Emma Jane Perkins went along on the trip. Like her husband, Sara Cobb was very taken with Rebecca who she thought was one of the smartest and most interesting young girls she'd ever met.

"I ain't sure, but she's going to turn out to be someone remarkable—a singer, or a writer, or a lady doctor," Sara Cobb predicted that night after they returned home. "Rebecca sure was good company. Why, there wasn't a dull moment all day."

Just before Thanksgiving, Rebecca became involved in a project helping the Simpson children that proved just how remarkable she was already.

From her first day at school, the girl from Sunnybrook Farm had felt a kinship with the large rowdy Simpson family who were desperately poor and struggled constantly just to make ends meet. Many was the time the children had to depend upon their neighbors just for scraps of food.

Mrs. Cobb and Emma Jane Went Along, Too.

The head of the clan, Abner Simpson, had the unfortunate habit of stealing farm tools and vehicles from one neighbor and swapping them for similar items that caught his fancy with another neighbor. Inevitably, the bungling thief got caught and ended up in jail. Mr. Simpson spent much of his time behind bars, while his poor wife spent her days taking in washing and cleaning other people's houses. Their six children did chores and helped out as best they could.

Despite their youth, Clara Belle and Susan Simpson had considerably more business sense than their foolish, ne'er-do-well father. That fall they came up with the bright idea of working for the Excelsior Soap Company and selling soap to their neighbors. However, the company did not pay wages. Instead, it awarded its salespeople a premium or a prize when they had sold a certain number of cakes of soap.

The Simpson sisters were so successful at

The Bright Idea of Selling Soap

selling that they quickly reached their goal and were awarded a child's handcart which they discovered worked well on bumpy country roads.

Armed with circulars featuring brightly colored pictures of the company's product, Clara Belle and Susan approached their new classmate, Rebecca, and asked her to join them in their business venture. The idea was to work hard together to earn a brass table lamp and shade for the Simpson home.

Carefully the Simpson girls explained how they planned to expand their operations by calling on new customers in nearby towns. Rebecca was so enthusiastic that she not only promised to be a saleswoman herself, but she persuaded Emma Jane to be her partner as well.

Before they set out on their route together the two friends memorized all the major points in the soap company's circular and practiced their sales talk in Emma Jane's attic. Emma

They Approached Their New Classmate.

Jane practiced her speech on Rebecca, and Rebecca, hers on Emma Jane.

"Can I sell you some soap this afternoon, madam?" Rebecca said with a dramatic flourish of her arms. "I have two kinds—Snow White for the laundry and Red Rose for the bath. Twenty cents a cake for the white and twenty-five for the red. Six cakes in each fancy box. I guarantee you that our soap is made from the purest ingredients and could even be eaten by a baby."

"Oh, Rebecca, don't say that," interrupted Emma Jane from the depths of an old moth-eaten settee where she was watching her friend's performance. "It makes me feel like a fool."

"I takes so little to make you feel like a fool, Emma Jane, that sometimes I think you must be one," Rebecca teased, plopping down on a wooden sled. "Well, maybe I ought to leave out the part about the baby eating the soap. Why don't you take over now?"

Practicing Their Speeches

"The Snow White is probably the most unusual soap ever manufactured," Emma Jane began as she took her turn on the dusty floor. "All you have to do is soak your clothes in a tub of sudsy water from sunrise to sunset, and even the youngest baby can wash them."

"I can't imagine a baby doing a family wash with any soap," Rebecca laughed, "but it must be true or the soap company wouldn't dare print it. At the houses where they don't know me, I won't be nervous at all. I will just reel off the whole rigmarole—even the part about the baby. Oh, I can't wait to get started."

Since Rebecca's aunts had gone to Portland to a funeral, she spent the weekend at Emma Jane's house. On Saturday, the girls planned to drive to North Riverboro, three miles away, to have lunch with Emma Jane's cousins at twelve o'clock and return by four.

When they asked Mrs. Perkins if they could call at a few houses going and coming to sell soap for the Simpsons, the dear lady finally

"I Can't Wait to Get Started."

agreed. Like everyone else in town, Mrs. Perkins had a tender spot in her heart for this poor family.

On a glorious Indian summer day, Emma Jane and Rebecca set out in the Perkins' horse and wagon and headed right to the Riverboro General Store to stock up on the Excelsior Company's soap, which they charged to Clara Belle Simpson's account.

Chatting happily, the two girls climbed back in the wagon and drove down the road toward North Riverboro. Trees, ablaze with the magnificent colors of autumn, lined the lane on either side.

"Whoa, Nellie," Emma Jane called suddenly to her beautiful white horse as they approached a weather-beaten salt box house that had been built right on the road. "All right, Rebecca, you couldn't wait to get started selling, so you can make the first sales call."

"Wish me luck," Rebecca said, as she jumped down from the wagon and picked out two

Setting Out in the Horse and Wagon

boxes of soap from the back. "After all, Clara Belle and Susan are depending on us."

Hurriedly, she walked up the front path and knocked on the door of the house. Somewhere above her, she heard a window fly open.

"Go away, little girl," a woman with a loud shrill voice called out. "Whatever you have in those boxes, I don't want any. Go away, you hear!"

"Go Away, Little Girl!"

Rebecca Hopped Aboard.

Chapter Seven

Two Remarkable People Meet

Trembling and fighting the tears after the encounter with the shrewish housewife, Rebecca rushed back to the wagon and hopped aboard without so much as a backward glance.

"Don't blame yourself," Emma Jane said when her distraught friend told her what had happened. "You didn't say or do anything wrong. It was just bad luck. I'm sure things will turn out differently next time."

"Oh, you make me feel better, Emma Jane," Rebecca replied gratefully, relaxing now. "You really are a good friend."

Anxious to make a success of her business venture, Rebecca insisted on being the one to call at the next house where they stopped. This time she received a warm welcome and sold a whole box of soap.

From then on, she sold soap to every customer she approached. Unfortunately, Emma Jane didn't fare as well. She only parted with three cakes all morning, while Rebecca sold three boxes.

"It's your turn, Rebecca, and I'm glad, too," said Emma Jane, drawing up to the gate of a house that was set back a good distance from the road. "Look. The blinds are all shut in the front. Maybe no one is home."

Rebecca walked up the lane to the house and went around to the side door. Seated in a rocking chair on the porch was a good-looking young man busy husking corn. His well-trimmed mustache and fashionable clothes gave him an air of sophistication.

Suddenly, Rebecca felt a trifle shy, but she

A Whole Box of Soap

knew she had to say something. "Is the lady of the house at home?"

"I am the lady of the house at present," answered the stranger with a grin. "What can I do for you?"

"Have you ever heard of the—would you like, or I mean—do you need any soap?" asked Rebecca.

"Do I look as if I did?" the young man responded unexpectedly.

"I didn't mean that. I have some soap to sell. I mean I would like to introduce you to a very remarkable soap. It's called the—"

"Oh, I know that soap," her customer interrupted. "Made out of pure vegetable fats, isn't it?"

"The very purest," Rebecca agreed.

"No acid in it?"

"Not a trace."

"And yet a child could do the Monday wash with it easily," the young man continued.

"A baby," corrected Rebecca, amazed to find

"Is the Lady of the House at Home?"

a customer who knew all her product's good points.

"Please have a seat," the stranger said graciously.

Rebecca sat down on a stool near the edge of the porch and finished her sales talk. The first thing she knew she had forgotten all about Emma Jane waiting patiently in the wagon with Nellie. Somehow, she felt as if she had known this charming man all her life.

"I'm taking care of the house today, but I don't live here," the young man explained. "I'm visiting my aunt who has gone on a trip to Portland. I used to visit her a great deal as a boy, and I'm very fond of the spot. Now tell me. How much soap do you think I should buy?"

"How much soap does your aunt have on hand?" Rebecca inquired, teetering back and forth on the rickety stool. "How much does she need?"

"Oh, I don't know," her customer answered. "Soap keeps, doesn't it?"

Rebecca Sat Down on a Stool.

"I'm not sure," said Rebecca conscientiously, "but I'll look in the circular. It's sure to tell." With that, she pulled the brochure from her pocket and began to thumb through it looking for the answer.

"What are you going to do with all the money you make from this business?" the young man asked. He had finished his job shucking corn and wiped his hands clean with an old tea towel.

"We are not working to make money for ourselves," Rebecca explained confidentially. "My friend Emma Jane and I are trying to help Clara Belle and Susan Simpson earn a premium—actually a banquet lamp—for their home. The Simpsons are poor as church mice, I'm afraid. They really need something to brighten up their life."

"It seems to me the Simpsons ought to have this banquet lamp if they want it, and you want them to have it," her new friend remarked, pacing the floor of the porch. "Let's do

"What Will You Do with the Money?"

some figuring. How much does the family lack at the moment?"

"If they sell two hundred more cakes this month and next, they will get the lamp by Christmas," Rebecca answered, "and they can get the shade by summer. However, I probably won't be able to help much after today because Aunt Miranda may not let me."

"I see. Well, then I'll take three hundred cakes," the young man said, "and that will give the Simpsons the shade and all."

"Goodness gracious!" Rebecca gasped. Overcome by shock and disbelief, she tipped back on her stool and fell off the porch into a clump of lilac bushes.

"Oh, let me help you," her host cried, as he jumped off the porch to the ground below. Quickly, he picked Rebecca up, set her on her feet, and brushed her off. "You should never seem surprised when you receive a large order. You should have asked if I would like to make it three hundred and fifty cakes instead of cap-

"I'll Take Three Hundred Cakes."

sizing in that very unbusinesslike way."

"Oh, I could never say anything like that," replied Rebecca, who was blushing now because of her awkward fall, "but it doesn't seem right for you to buy so much. Are you sure you can afford it?"

"If I can't, I'll save on something else," replied her best customer.

"What if your aunt doesn't like this kind of soap?" queried Rebecca nervously.

"My aunt always likes what I like," he said.

"Mine doesn't!" exclaimed Rebecca.

"Then there's something wrong with your aunt."

"Or with me," laughed the very successful young saleswoman.

"What is your name, young lady?"

"Rebecca Rowena Randall, sir."

"Do you want to know my name?" he asked.

"I think I know it already," answered Rebecca brightly. "I'm sure you must be Mr. Aladdin of the *Arabian Nights*. Oh, please, can I

"Are You Sure You Can Afford It?"

run down and tell Emma Jane the good news? She must be tired of waiting, and she will be so glad."

"Yes, you go right ahead," Mr. Aladdin said.

Rebecca flew down the lane as fast as her legs would carry her. "Emma Jane! Emma Jane!" she cried, rushing up to the wagon and giving Nellie a big hug around her neck. "We are all sold out! Mr. Aladdin brought three hundred cakes of soap—enough for us to get the lamp and the shade for the Simpsons at the same time. Isn't that unbelieveable?"

A Hug for Nellie

"It Would Be a Nice Surprise."

Chapter 8

Thanksgiving Surprises

"It's the truth—every word of it," said Mr. Aladdin who had followed Rebecca out to the wagon to verify the astonishing news of her big sale. "If you two girls could keep a secret, it would be a nice surprise to have the lamp arrive at the Simpsons' home on Thanksgiving Day. Let me have your circular, and I'll write the Excelsior Soap Company tonight to see if I can arrange it."

As Mr. Aladdin talked, he lifted the boxes of soap from the back of the wagon and stacked them on the ground. Then he tucked the lap robe around Emma Jane and Rebecca's feet, so that they would be warm and cozy on their trip home.

Tears of joy flooded Rebecca's eyes. "Oh, thank you, Mr. Aladdin," she said. "We really appreciate all you're doing to help us."

"Yes, we do. Thank you so much for everything," Emma Jane chimed in happily.

"Don't mention it!" laughed Mr. Aladdin, lifting his hat. "I like to see things done well. Good-bye, Miss Rebecca Rowena Randall. Just let me know whenever you have anything to sell because you can be sure I'll want it."

"Good-bye, Mr. Aladdin! I surely will," cried the young saleswoman, tossing back her dark braids and waving her hand as they drove away.

"Oh, my," said Emma Jane in an awe-struck whisper, "he tipped his hat to us, and we're not thirteen. It will be five years before we're ladies."

"Never mind," answered Rebecca, enjoying

"He Tipped His Hat!"

every moment of her success. "We are the beginning of ladies, even now."

"Wasn't it nice of him to buy us out?" Emma Jane continued ecstatically. "Just think. We got both the lamp and the shade for one day's work. Now what was that man's name?"

"I never thought to ask," Rebecca admitted. "I called him Mr. Aladdin because he made it possible for us to get the lamp. You remember the story of Aladdin and the wonderful lamp?"

"Oh, Rebecca, how could you call him by a nickname the first time you met him?" Emma Jane scolded.

"Mr. Aladdin isn't really a nickname," Rebecca replied. "Anyway he laughed and seemed to enjoy it."

It was no easy task, but Rebecca and Emma Jane sealed their lips and kept their exciting news to themselves until Thanksgiving Day finally arrived.

That morning, the lamp and shade were delivered to the Simpson house in a large pack-

"We Are the Beginning of Ladies, Even Now."

ing box. One of the boys, "Seesaw" Simpson, who had earned his nickname because he had trouble making up his mind, unpacked the lamp and set it up on a table for his excited family to see. Secretly, he had to admit to himself that he was mighty impressed with the business ability of his sisters, Clara Belle and Susan.

While the Simpsons began their Thanksgiving celebration on this high note, Rebecca spent a quiet day with her aunts, Miranda and Jane, and their guests. Keeping up an old tradition, the Burnham sisters, who lived between North Riverboro and Shaker Village, had driven over especially for the occasion.

After dinner was over and the dishes were washed, Rebecca sat in the parlor and read a book. When it was nearly five, she asked if she might go visit the Simpsons.

"Why do you want to run after those Simpson children on Thanksgiving Day?" Miranda barked. "Can't you sit still for once and listen

"Seesaw" Simpson Unpacked the Lamp.

to the conversation of your elders?"

"The Simpson family have a new lamp, and Emma Jane and I promised to go over and see it lighted," Rebecca answered patiently, putting down her book. "We want to make it kind of a party."

"Where on earth did they get the money for a lamp?" Miranda inquired. "If Abner were at home, I would guess he'd been swapping again."

"The children got it as a prize for selling soap," explained Rebecca. "You know I told you that Emma Jane and I helped them the Saturday afternoon you were in Portland."

"I didn't take notice, I suppose. This is the first time I ever heard the lamp mentioned," her aunt commented haughtily. "Well, you can go to the Simpsons' for an hour, and no more. What have you got in the pocket of that dress that makes it sag down so?"

"It's my nuts and raisins from dinner," stammered Rebecca. "I thought if I saved them for

"I Promised to See It Lighted."

the Simpsons, it would make their party better."

"They were yours, Rebecca," interrupted Jane Sawyer, "and if you chose to save them to give away, it is all right. We should never let this day pass without giving our neighbors something to be thankful for."

The Burnham sisters nodded approvingly as Rebecca left and remarked that they had never seen a child grow and improve so fast in so short a time.

"There's plenty of room left for improvement," Miranda snapped. "Of all the foolishness I ever heard of, that lamp beats everything. I didn't think those Simpson children had brains enough to sell anything."

"One of them must have," said Ellen Burnham with a twinkle in her eye. "Adam Ladd said the girl he bought the soap from was the most remarkable child he'd ever met."

"It must have been Clara Belle, but I would hardly call her remarkable," Miranda said sar-

"They Were Yours, Rebecca."

castically. "Has Adam been home again?"

"Yes, he's been staying a few days with his aunt," Ellen said, helping herself to some chocolate mints in a candy dish. "I hear tell he has lots of money. Strange, he's never married, being so fond of children and all."

"There's hope for him still, though," said Jane smiling. "I don't suppose he's more than thirty."

"He could get a wife in Riverboro if he was a hundred and thirty," remarked Miranda in a rare display of humor.

"Adam's aunt says he was so taken with the little girl that sold him the soap—Clara Belle did you say her name was?—that he said he was going to give her a Christmas present," Ellen continued, munching on another piece of chocolate candy.

"Well, there's no accounting for taste," exclaimed Miranda. "Clara Belle is cross-eyed and has red hair, but I'd be the last one to begrudge her a Christmas present. The more

"Strange, He's Never Married."

Adam Ladd gives to her the less the town will have to."

"Isn't there another Simpson girl?" asked Lydia Burnham. "This one couldn't have been cross-eyed. I remember Mrs. Ladd saying that Adam told her it was the child's beautiful eyes that made him buy three hundred cakes of soap. Mrs. Ladd has it all stacked outside in her shed."

"Three hundred cakes!" cried Miranda. "Well, there's one crop that never fails in Riverboro."

"What's that?" asked Lydia, wide-eyed.

"The fool crop," responded Miranda indignantly and changed the subject, much to Jane's relief.

For the last fifteen minutes, Jane had been increasingly nervous and ill at ease. Finally, she sat down on a tall, straight-backed chair to ponder this startling news. "What child in Riverboro could be described as remarkable except Rebecca?" she asked herself. "What

"The Fool Crop," Said Miranda.

child in town has particularly beautiful eyes except Rebecca? And what child had enough gumption to persuade a grown man to buy cakes of soap by the hundred except her rather persuasive niece?"

Meanwhile, the "remarkable" child had flown up the road to the Simpsons' house. She hadn't gone far when she heard the sound of footsteps in the distance and saw Emma Jane coming in her direction.

"Oh, Rebecca," Emma Jane cried, grabbing her friend by the hands. "I hate to tell you bad news, but something terrible has happened over at the Simpsons'!"

Up the Road to the Simpsons'

"No Kerosene and No Wicks."

Chapter 9

A Christmas to Remember

"Don't tell me the lamp is broken?" Rebecca asked Emma Jane when they met just a stone's throw from the Simpsons' property.

"No! Oh, no! Not that!" Emma Jane assured her. "The lamp was packed in straw and was in perfect condition when Seesaw unpacked it."

"Then what's wrong?" Rebecca cried, as the two girls raced into the Simpsons' yard and up the front walk.

"The problem is that Mr. and Mrs. Simpson have no kerosene and no wicks," Emma Jane

133

explained. "Seesaw has gone to the doctor's to see if he can borrow a wick. Mother loaned them a pint of oil, but she says she can't spare any more. You know, we never considered the expense of keeping up the lamp, Rebecca."

Once the girls arrived at the Simpsons', they were delighted to see that Seesaw had been successful in his search for a wick. The lamp had been placed on a table in the far corner of the living room and was illuminating the first floor with a soft golden glow. Never had Emma Jane and Rebecca seen the Simpson clan so happy and thrilled as they were about this new addition to their home.

For the two fast friends, it was their best Thanksgiving ever, for they knew it was their hard work that had made this day possible for this needy family. Finally, at six o'clock, Rebecca announced she had to go home.

"I'm so glad you and Emma Jane live where you can see the lamp shine from our windows," Clara Belle told Rebecca. "I only hope I can

The Simpson Clan Happy and Thrilled

light the lamp for at least one hour every night."

"You won't have to worry about kerosene any more," Seesaw announced, coming in from the shed. "Mr. Tubbs just delivered a large keg of it. It was a gift from someone up in North Riverboro."

"Mr. Aladdin, who else?" Rebecca whispered to Emma Jane. "Wasn't that nice of him? Now the Simpsons can enjoy the lamp to their hearts' content."

When Rebecca returned home to the brick house, the Burnham sisters had left, and her aunts were knitting in the parlor.

"It was a heavenly party," the happy young girl sighed, waltzing in the front door and spinning around the room. "Oh, Aunt Jane, Aunt Miranda, if you'll only come in the kitchen and look out the window, you will see the banquet lamp shining all red, just as if the Simpsons' house was on fire."

"It probably will be before long," observed

Her Aunts Were Knitting in the Parlor.

Miranda wryly. "I've got no patience with such foolish goin's-on."

Jane followed her niece into the kitchen. "Rebecca, who was it that sold three hundred cakes of soap to Mr. Ladd in North Riverboro?"

"Mr. Who?" exclaimed Rebecca.

"Mr. Ladd in North Riverboro."

"Is that his real name?" asked Rebecca in astonishment. "I didn't make a bad guess." And she laughed softly to herself.

"I asked you who sold the soap to Adam Ladd?" Jane pressed on.

"Oh, Aunt Jane, the truth is that Emma Jane and I did."

"Did you tease him or make him buy it?" her aunt probed, frowning.

"Now, Aunt Jane, how could I make a big grownup man buy anything if he didn't want to? He needed the soap dreadfully as a present for his aunt," Rebecca replied.

"Oh, child, you look as if you have a lamp burning inside you," sighed Jane Sawyer, who

"Who Sold 300 Cakes of Soap?"

was still somewhat unconvinced as to her niece's tactics. "You must take life easier. I do worry about you."

Jane Sawyer's fears about her niece proved to be groundless, for Rebecca was a plucky and optimistic girl, who immediately put all her energy into preparations for Christmas. For weeks in advance, she busied herself making presents for her two aunts and her family at Sunnybrook Farm. On December 22, she got her box of presents off to Temperance on the stage.

At last Christmas Day arrived. It was a fresh crystal-clear morning, with icicles hanging like dazzling pendants from the trees and a glaze of pale blue on the surface of the snow. The Simpsons' red barn stood out, a glowing mass of color in the white landscape.

Shortly after eight o'clock, Rebecca and her aunts gathered in the parlor near the tall spruce tree, decorated with popcorn and hand-made ornaments, and exchanged presents.

At Last Christmas Day arrived.

Rebecca received a somewhat unbecoming gray squirrel muff from Miranda, a lovely green cashmere dress from Jane, a crocheted collar from her mother, and red wool mittens from the Cobbs.

Just as her aunts were opening the teacozies Rebecca had made them, there was a knock at the door. There on the front steps stood a young boy with a package for Rebecca.

"It must be a present," said the dazed girl, examining the parcel carefully. "I can't think who it could be from."

The package contained two small gifts. With trembling fingers, Rebecca opened the one addressed to her. "Oh, how beautiful," she cried, holding up a long chain of delicate pink coral beads with a cross made of coral rosebuds. In the box was a card that read, "Merry Christmas from Mr. Aladdin."

"Of all things!" exclaimed Rebecca's surprised aunts, rising in their seats. "Who sent it?"

A Package for Rebecca

"Mr. Ladd," said Rebecca under her breath. "Adam Ladd! Well, I never! Don't you remember Ellen Burnham said he was going to send Rebecca a Christmas present. But I never supposed he'd think of it again," said Jane. "What's the other package?"

"It's for Emma Jane," replied Rebecca. "Wasn't it nice of Mr. Ladd to remember us both?"

"Look, dear, there's a letter," Jane pointed out. "What does it say?"

Choking back the tears, Rebecca stood before her aunts and read the note from Mr. Ladd aloud.

Dear Miss Rebecca Rowena Randall,
My idea of a Christmas present is something entirely unnecessary. I have always noticed when I give this sort of thing that people love it, so I hope I have not chosen wrong for you and your friend. You must wear your chain this afternoon for me to see. I am coming over

"What Does the Letter Say?"

in my new sleigh to take you and Emma Jane for a drive. My aunt is delighted with the soap.

Sincerely your friend,
Adam Ladd

"Well, well!" cried Jane, "wasn't that kind of Adam Ladd? Now eat your breakfast, Rebecca, and after we've done the dishes, you can run over to Emma Jane's and deliver her present."

True to his word, Mr. Ladd came to call at the brick house that afternoon. Jane and Miranda ushered him into the parlor where they sat and made polite conversation.

Wearing her new green cashmere dress and exquisite coral necklace, Rebecca perched rigidly on a footstool near the crackling fire. Silent and shy, she could hardly utter a word. Yet inwardly she was bursting with happiness. No one had ever made such a fuss over her before, and she was deeply touched.

"Are you ready for a ride in my sleigh, Rebecca?" Mr. Ladd said finally, offering her his

Mr. Ladd Came to Call.

hand and helping her to her feet.

"Oh, yes," the excited girl cried. "I've been looking forward to this all day."

Suddenly, Rebecca began to relax and enjoy herself. All afternoon as this charming man drove her and Emma Jane around the frozen countryside, she chatted away like a magpie. When the starry-eyed child returned home at dusk, she vowed she would remember this glorious Christmas Day as long as she lived.

That night when she was drifting off to sleep with the precious coral necklace under her pillow, Rebecca relived all the exciting events of the holiday season. "What does the future hold in store for me?" she wondered. "Oh, I do hope the new year will be a good one."

They Drove Around the Frozen Countryside.

Certain Milestones Stood Out.

Chapter Ten

Challenging Times

When Rebecca looked back upon the year or two that followed the Simpsons' Thanksgiving party, certain important milestones stood out in her memory.

To begin with, the saga of the Simpson family took a surprising turn. To the shock of everyone in Riverboro, Abner Simpson moved his family, bag and baggage, to Bridgewater.

In spite of all the security precautions that were taken, a pulpit chair, several kerosene lamps, and a small stove disappeared mysteriously from the Riverboro Church. While no

151

one could prove it, folks were certain that Abner had stolen these items to swap with his new neighbors in Bridgewater.

Not long afterward, Rebecca and Emma Jane were stunned to learn that the minister of the Bridgewater Church had acquired a magnificent brass banquet lamp which he placed in the church parlor.

Gossip had it that Abner had been spotted peddling hurriedly out of town on an old, rickety bicycle that belonged to the minister. Apparently his family were so up in arms about the disappearance of their precious lamp that Abner didn't dare return home for many a day.

Despite her dismay regarding Abner's latest misdeed, Rebecca took comfort in knowing she had done everything she could to help the poor unfortunate Simpson brood. For her, the biggest loss was her friendship with Clara Belle and Susan. Oh, how she missed their good times together.

The year was also notable for being the one

Spotted on an Old Rickety Bicycle

in which Rebecca shot up like a young tree. Jane Sawyer spent days lengthening the hems and sleeves in all her niece's dresses, so she could get more wear out of them. Eventually, the clothes were boxed up and sent to Sunnybrook Farm to be made over for Jenny.

It was also the year when a terrible tragedy occurred at Sunnybrook Farm. Mira, the baby of the Randall family, died suddenly, and Rebecca went home for a two week visit.

The homecoming was a sad one for this warm and loving girl. Mira had been her special charge from the moment she was born. In her grief, Rebecca had to face not only the loss of her baby sister but a host of new thoughts about the mystery of death. It broke her heart to observe her mother's suffering—particularly when Mrs. Randall had worked so hard to keep her family together all these years.

Normally, her brother John would have cheered up Rebecca, but he was no longer living at Sunnybrook Farm. Cousin Ann's hus-

A Sad Homecoming

band had died, and John had gone to reside with her and be the man of the house.

Rebecca spent her spare time exploring the farm and visiting the haunts of her early childhood. One morning she stopped by the maple tree where she had found the oriole's nest, the hedge that housed a nimble little brown field mouse, and the moss-covered stump that overlooked a clump of white toadstools which had sprung up as if by magic.

Another day, she called to pay her respects to the ancient and honorable toad who lived in a hole at the root of an old pine tree and then she wandered by the dear little sunny brook she loved so much.

There was no laughing water sparkling in the winter sun that afternoon. Now, like Mira, the creek was cold and quiet, wrapped in a blanket of snow. But it was all right! Sunnybrook would sing again in the spring.

In her travels, Rebecca thought constantly about her sister, Hannah, who had worked so

Haunts of Her Early Childhood

hard to help her mother all these years. Although life at the brick house in Riverboro had not been a bed of roses, Rebecca had had the opportunity to attend a good school and make some wonderful friends. She realized that she had been very fortunate indeed.

Now Rebecca was willing to make a tremendous sacrifice for Hannah's sake. Many tears were shed as she agonized over this decision.

Then one morning as her visit neared its end, Rebecca finally spoke up. "Hannah, after this term, I'm going to come home and let you go away. Aunt Miranda has always wanted you. It's only fair you should have your turn."

Hannah was darning stockings, and she threaded her needle and snipped off the yarn before she answered. "No, thank you, Becky. Mother couldn't manage without me, and besides I love it here. I'm not one to be lonesome." As she spoke, she blushed, but her sister was not to know why for another year or two.

Rebecca could see that Hannah meant what

Rebecca Spoke Up.

she said and returned to Riverboro intent upon pursuing her studies diligently. Spring and summer arrived, bringing happier times for the sensitive young girl. Gradually, she began to recover from her sister's death.

That fall another milestone occurred in Rebecca's life. This time it was a happy event and one she had looked forward to for a long time.

Rebecca entered Wareham Academy with the intention of completing the four year course in three years. According to her plan, she would be seventeen when she graduated and would then be in a position to earn a living and help educate her younger brothers and sisters.

Rebecca continued to live at the brick house and to travel to the town of Wareham every day by train. Her aunts thought it would be a good idea for her to take the train from September to Christmas and then live in Wareham during the three coldest months. Rebecca was even happier that Emma Jane was a

Rebecca Entered Wareham Academy.

student at the Academy, too.

Among the teachers at Wareham Academy was one who influenced Rebecca tremendously. Miss Emily Maxwell, the daughter of a Bowdoin College professor, taught English literature and composition and was a published writer.

One day during a class discussion, Miss Maxwell asked each new pupil to bring her a composition written in the last year, so that she might judge their work.

Rebecca lingered after the others and approached the teacher's desk shyly. "My compositions are all packed away in a box in the attic, Miss Maxwell. I don't think they're too good. What I really like to write is poetry."

"Poetry!" Miss Maxwell exclaimed. "Did Miss Dearborn require you to write it?"

"Oh, no," Rebecca cried. "I have always written poetry even at the farm. I'll bring some poems in for you to read tomorrow."

The next day, Rebecca took the blank book

Rebecca Approached Miss Maxwell's Desk.

which contained her work and left it at Miss Maxwell's house. She very much hoped she would be invited in and would have a chance to talk to her teacher about her poetry. However, a housekeeper answered the door, and Rebecca walked away disappointed.

Several days later, Rebecca saw her blank book on Miss Maxwell's desk, so she was not surprised when she was asked to stay after school.

The room was quiet. Red leaves rustled in the breeze and flew in the open window. Miss Maxwell walked over and sat down beside Rebecca on the bench.

"Did you think your poems were good?" she asked, handing her student her book.

"Not really," confessed Rebecca, sitting rigidly on the bench in nervous anticipation. Beneath her dress she could feel her heart flutter. "But it's hard to tell by yourself. The Perkinses and the Cobbs always said they were wonderful. However, when Mrs. Cobb

A Housekeeper Answered the Door.

told me she thought they were better than Longfellow's, I was worried. I knew that couldn't be true. However, the most important opinion is yours, Miss Maxwell. Did you like my poems? Did you think they were good?"

"Did You Like My Poems?"

"Then I Must Give Up All Hope."

Chapter Eleven

An Understanding Heart

"Well, Rebecca," Miss Maxwell said, feeling certain that this was a bright student who could handle constructive criticism well, "your friends were wrong, and you were right. Your poems are pretty bad." She looked directly at Rebecca and smiled as she spoke to soften her remark.

"Then I must give up all hope of ever being a writer," sighed Rebecca, praying that she could hold the tears back until the interview was over.

"I wouldn't go that far," interrupted her

teacher. "Though they don't amount to much as poetry, they show a good deal of promise in other directions. You almost never make a mistake in rhyme or meter, and this shows you have a natural sense of what is right—a sense of form, poets call it. When you are older and have more knowledge, experience, and vision, which poetry requires, I think you may write very good verse. Of course, you already have imagination. That's very important, too."

"Should I never write poetry again, not even to amuse myself?" Rebecca asked quietly.

"Of course you should continue to write poetry," Miss Maxwell replied encouragingly. "It will help you write better prose. Now for the first composition, I am going to ask all the new students to write a letter giving a description of the town and their impression of school life here."

"Do I have to be myself?" asked Rebecca, feeling a bit more cheerful.

"What do you mean?"

"You Almost Never Make a Mistake."

"A letter from Rebecca Randall to her sister Hannah at Sunnybrook Farm or Aunt Jane in Riverboro would be a little dull, but if I could pretend I was a different girl, it would be so exciting."

"That's a very creative idea," exclaimed her teacher. "Who would you like to be?"

"Oh, an heiress I think," replied Rebecca in a dreamy mood now. "Of course, I never saw one, but interesting things are always happening to heiresses. My heiress would go to a good school in Boston and have a guardian because her father died. Yes, the girl shall be called Evelyn Abercrombie, and her guardian shall be Mr. Adam Ladd."

"Do you know Mr. Ladd?" asked her teacher in surprise.

"He's my best friend," cried Rebecca gaily. "Do you know him, too?"

"Yes, he's a trustee of the school and comes here often."

"I see," said Rebecca thoughtfully. "I hope

"Do You Know Mr. Ladd?"

he'll come by to see me one of these days."

The first winter when Rebecca became a boarder at the Academy was the happiest time of her school days. She enjoyed all her classes and loved being roommates with Emma Jane. The two girls worked hard to make their quarters cozy and attractive.

To begin with, the room was furnished with a set of maple furniture and a bright red carpet. Mrs. Perkins worked long and hard to make the girls curtains and bedspreads of unbleached muslin which she trimmed with red cotton.

Each girl had her own study corner with a lamp. After Christmas, they added the wonderful presents Mr. Ladd gave them—a Japanese screen for Emma Jane and a set of books by the English poets for Rebecca.

One snowy January afternoon as Rebecca was studying alone in her room, she heard a noise outside in the hall. The door opened softly, and a voice called out, "Emily Maxwell told

Their Cozy and Attractive Quarters

me I could find Miss Rebecca Randall here."

"Mr. Aladdin!" cried Rebecca, slamming her book shut and springing to her feet. "I didn't know you were in Wareham. I'm so glad to see you. Please come in and make yourself at home."

The light in the room grew softer, and the fire crackled cheerily as these two old friends chatted away. They had not seen each other in several months and had to catch up on each other's news. Mr. Ladd was delighted to hear from his young friend how happy she was in school. Miss Maxwell had told him she was doing well in her studies and had become a leader in her class.

"Rebecca, this had all been very nice," Mr. Ladd said finally, "but I must be going. I have a long drive to Portland to attend a meeting of railroad directors tomorrow. I did want to drop by and check into the Academy's educational and financial affairs, though."

"It seems funny for you to be a school

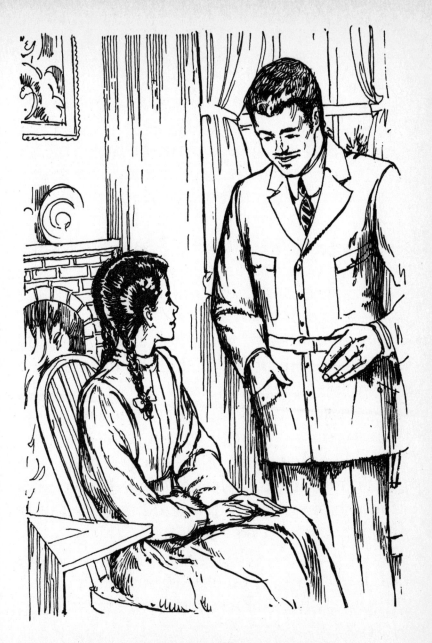

Two Old Friends Chatted Away.

trustee," said Rebecca, stoking the fire. "I can't quite make it fit somehow."

"I accepted the position in memory of my mother who died when I was ten. She was a student here when she was a young girl, you see."

"That was a long time ago," said Rebecca.

"Let me see. I am thirty-two—thirty-two despite an occasional gray hair. Would you like to see a picture of my mother?"

Rebecca opened the leather case Mr. Ladd handed her and gazed at the photograph of a very pretty young woman with golden curls. "What a sweet face," she whispered softly.

"I'm afraid she had to bear a lot of storms," Mr. Ladd said gravely. "I was only a child and could do nothing to help her. Now I have success and money, all that would have made life easier for her, and it's too late."

This was a new side to Adam Ladd that Rebecca had never seen before, and her heart went out to him. "I'm so glad I know about

Rebecca Opened the Leather Case.

this," she said. "I know your mother would be very proud of you if she were alive today."

"Goodbye, Miss Rebecca Randall," said Mr. Ladd, taking her slim hands in his and looking into her eyes, as if he were seeing her for the first time, "you are a great comfort to me. It's not every fifteen year old girl who would be so understanding."

"Oh, I do understand," Rebecca replied, as she showed Mr. Ladd to the door. Her eyes filled with tears as she spoke. "My father died when I was just a little girl, and my mother has had a terrible financial struggle trying to raise us. Not only that, but now I'm worried about Aunt Jane and Aunt Miranda. I have this feeling something's wrong, but I don't know what it is. I'll just have to keep my mind on my work, and try to find out."

The school year sped happily by for Rebecca. That summer she studied diligently and on her return to the Academy in the fall, she took and passed the exams that would enable her

"You Are a Great Comfort to Me."

to complete her high school course in three years, as she had planned, instead of four. Rebecca's early graduation was now virtually assured.

Unfortunately, the situation at the brick house in Riverboro was more difficult than ever. Her Aunt Miranda was always quick to anger. Never before had she been so critical and sarcastic.

One Saturday after a stormy scene in the kitchen, Rebecca ran upstairs in tears and sobbed, "Oh, Aunt Jane, there's no pleasing Aunt Miranda. Everything I do is wrong. She just said it will take my whole life to get the Randall out of me. I'm not sure I want to do that. So there!"

Jane Sawyer put her arms around Rebecca and held her close. Then she leaned back and wiped the tears from her niece's eyes with her handkerchief. "You must be patient with Miranda," she said. "I haven't told you this because I didn't want to worry you when you

"Be Patient with Miranda."

were studying so hard, but your Aunt Miranda isn't well."

"Isn't well? What's wrong, Aunt Jane?" Rebecca cried. "You know I've suspected something all along."

"About a month ago, Miranda had a fainting spell. The doctor wasn't sure if it was a stroke or not, but if it was, then it's a very serious matter. Personally, I think she's been failing for some time. That's what makes her so irritable, you see. Miranda has other troubles, too, that you don't know about. You're going to have to be patient with her, Rebecca."

"Oh, Aunt Jane, this is so upsetting," an anguished Rebecca cried as she grabbed her aunt by the hands. "Of course, I'll do everything I can to be a good and loving niece to Aunt Miranda. But first, you must tell me what these mysterious troubles of hers are. I have to know!"

"What's Wrong, Aunt Jane?"

"Troubles with Money"

Chapter Twelve

A Heavy Load for
Young Shoulders

"I hate to tell you this, Rebecca, but I'm afraid Miranda's troubles and mine, too, for that matter, have to do with money," Jane explained in a worried tone of voice as they sat talking upstairs in the brick house. There was a frown on her face as she spoke, and she twisted her handkerchief nervously in her lap.

"What happened, Aunt Jane? Rebecca cried.

"Miranda invested twenty-five hundred dollars of our money in a business owned by a friend of our father," Jane began. "For years, we received an annual income of a hundred dollars. When father's friend died, his son took over the business. For five years everything ran smoothly. Then suddenly one day, we got a letter explaining that the firm had gone bankrupt, and we had lost all our money."

"Oh, how terrible!" Rebecca cried sympathetically, squeezing her aunt's hand. "So now, you don't have that hundred dollar income every year."

"That's right, and a hundred dollars was a lot of money to us. Of course, all this happened when we sent you to Wareham Academy, so we have really had to pinch our pennies," Jane went on.

"Did you have other investments?" Rebecca wanted to know.

"Yes, and we are living on the interest from that money. We don't ever want to dip into the principal," her aunt stated emphatically.

"I feel like such a burden," Rebecca said, tears welling in her eyes.

"Then Suddenly We Lost All Our Money!"

"You mustn't feel that way," Jane Sawyer assured her, giving her niece a hug and holding her close. "Your sister Hannah is involved with the young man she's seeing, and your brother John wants to be a doctor. The way we see it, you are Aurelia's only hope for the future. It's important you get your education, so you will be able to work when you graduate and help your mother support the younger children."

Unfortunately, things were not running smoothly at Sunnybrook Farm either. The potato crop had failed, and there were hardly any apples on the trees. The hay crop was a puny one, and Aurelia was having spells of dizziness. To make matters worse, Mark had broken his ankle. The time had come to pay the interest on the mortgage, and for the first time in fourteen years, the Randalls did not have the required forty-eight dollars.

The only bright spot on the horizon was Hannah's engagement to Will Melville, a

Not Smooth at Sunnybrook Farm

young farmer whose land adjoined Sunnybrook Farm. But Hannah was so wrapped up
in her own world that she hardly recognized
how nervous and upset her mother was about
money matters.

Right after the engagement was announced,
Hannah came to Riverboro to visit at the brick
house for a week. Rebecca enjoyed their time
together very much, but Miranda and Jane
were not as enthusiastic.

The afternoon Hannah took the stagecoach
back to Temperance, Miranda told Jane she
was glad to see her go. "She's a selfish girl,
that Hannah. She'll never do anything more to
help Aurelia with all those children. I spoke to
her about it just before she left."

"What did she say?" Jane asked, putting
some corn pudding she had made in the stove
as they chatted in the kitchen.

"She told me she'd done her share helping
her mother for years, and she wasn't going to
burden Will with her poor relations. Those

Hannah Came to Riverboro.

were her exact words," Miranda reported.

"Well, I never," Jane replied, genuinely shocked. She clutched the back of a chair to steady herself.

"She's a Randall through and through," Miranda snorted, as she headed in the dining room to set the table. "If that mortgage on Sunnybrook Farm is ever paid up, it won't be Hannah that'll do it. It'll be Rebecca or me!"

When Rebecca returned to the Academy that fall, she knew she had to study harder than ever because her family were all depending on her to make top grades and get a good job when she graduated.

Naturally, she was thrilled when her classmates elected her assistant editor of the school paper, "The Pilot." Not only was it a great honor, but it gave her an opportunity to write more essays and poems and see her work in print. And so it was, that the golden autumn days sped swiftly by.

One day when Adam Ladd was in Wareham,

"Well, I Never."

he stopped by school to see Rebecca. He had just been in Temperance on business connected with the proposed branch of the railroad that might possibly lead right through Sunnybrook Farm. If the deal took place, Mrs. Randall would receive a tidy sum of money for her land. Word had reached Mr. Ladd that this good lady was mighty pressed financially. He wondered how all this was affecting Rebecca.

As they strolled the campus together, Mr. Ladd couldn't help but notice that she looked pale and thin from all the long, hard hours of study. However, Rebecca was wearing a very attractive black wool dress that was her Aunt Jane's second best, and she had roped her braids around the back of her head in a very feminine style.

Adam Ladd looked at her in a way that made Rebecca put her hands over her face and laugh through them shyly. "I know what you're thinking," she said, "that my dress is an inch longer than last year and my hair is different,

They Strolled the Campus Together.

but I'm not a young lady yet. Truly I'm not. I'll be sixteen in one month."

"You look very nice," her dear friend said, "but I'm afraid you're working too hard. Perhaps you should rest up over vacation and try to recover your dimples."

A shadow crept over Rebecca's face. "Don't be kind, Mr. Aladdin. I can't bear it. It's not one of my dimply days." And she ran in the school gate and disappeared with a farewell wave of her hand.

Adam Ladd wended his way to the principal's office in a thoughtful mood. This year marked the fiftieth anniversary of the founding of Wareham Academy. He wanted to tell Mr. Morrison that, in addition to his gift of a hundred books to the reference library, he wanted to celebrate by offering prizes in English literature. The generous trustee had decided that the awards would be made to the writers of the two best essays submitted by students in the junior and senior classes. The

"Not One of My Dimply Days."

prizes would either be money or books.

After a very profitable interview with Mr. Morrison whereupon they made a lot of decisions, Mr. Ladd stopped by Emily Maxwell's office to tell her about the English literature competition and to discuss Rebecca.

"Doesn't it strike you that she looks wretchedly tired?" he asked.

"She does indeed, and I am considering taking her south with me to Old Point Comfort for a good rest during school vacation," Miss Maxwell told him. "The problem is I have a slender purse."

"You must let me help with the traveling expenses," Mr. Ladd offered, pacing the floor excitedly. "I would be so happy to do something to make life easier for Rebecca."

"I accept your kind offer," Miss Maxwell said, "but only on the condition that it must be a secret between the two of us. Are we in agreement?"

"We are," Mr. Ladd said, and the two friends

To Discuss Rebecca

shook hands warmly. "Maybe you could help Rebecca decide on the title for the essay she is going to write for the competition. I'm sure she will want to enter."

Right at that moment, Mr. Ladd and Miss Maxwell looked out the window and saw Rebecca walk by in the company of a tall, attractive boy of about sixteen. Apparently, they were reading something aloud, for their heads were bent over a sheet of paper. Rebecca kept glancing up at her friend, her eyes sparkling with appreciation.

"Miss Maxwell!" cried Mr. Ladd, "I am a trustee of this school, but upon my word, I don't believe in coeducation!"

"I have my doubts, too, from time to time," Miss Maxwell admitted, "but today's not one of them. That's a very impressive sight which you are privileged to witness. For the two young people who just walked by are the editor-in-chief and the assistant editor of our school paper, The Pilot.

They Saw Rebecca and a Boy Walk By.

What a Wonderful Time They Had!

Chapter Thirteen

A Bittersweet Graduation

In the end Emily Maxwell did invite Rebecca to go south with her to Old Point Comfort on a vacation. What a wonderful time they had! They walked the white sandy beach together, basked in the sun, and picked wildflowers in the woods nearby.

These two special friends, teacher and student, spent hours discussing music, art, literature, and of course, the essay competition. Rebecca felt so alive and refreshed that she even chose her topic, "Follow Your Saint", and wrote most of the essay.

Secretly, she thought she would never be happy unless she was chosen a winner. It was not the money she yearned for or even the honor; she wanted only to please Mr. Ladd and justify his belief in her.

The awards were announced at the fiftieth anniversary celebration held in late May in the school church. Looking back years later, Rebecca always felt that winning the essay competition her junior year was one of her greatest achievements at Wareham Academy.

Amidst great pomp and circumstance, the governor of Maine presented Rebecca and the other winner, a senior named Herbert Dunn, with the prize money. Each student received five ten dollar gold pieces.

Rebecca remembered that she was nervous and could feel her whole body tremble when she walked up to the podium and shook hands with the governor. She couldn't believe her eyes or her ears when Jeremiah Cobb, who had driven over for the day, jumped up, waved

Presenting Rebecca the Prize Money

his straw hat in the air, and shouted, "Hooray!"

The talented young writer was thrilled to win the award for Mr. Ladd's sake and for the sake of her family who set such store by her. The governor read her essay himself and wrote Jane and Miranda Sawyer a long letter praising their niece to the heights. Naturally, these two ladies were proud as peacocks. Aurelia Randall was proud, too, and grateful when her daughter gave her the prize money to pay the interest on the mortgage.

Rebecca's triumph at Wareham Academy created quite a stir in Riverboro. People talked about it over their teacups for months afterward.

No one was surprised when Rebecca went home to Sunnybrook Farm for the summer. Hannah had married Will Melville rather suddenly, and Mrs. Randall needed Rebecca to help run the house for a while.

That fall when Rebecca returned to the

A Long Letter Praising Their Niece

Academy, she plunged into her studies with a fervor. She was determined to make her senior year her best year yet.

It was a year spent conjugating French verbs, memorizing English poetry, studying American history and writing a series of good essays—several of which were printed with her by-line in "The Pilot."

Then spring burst upon the scene in a glory of tulips and daffodils. With it came the hectic week of examinations, which was the last hurdle Rebecca had to face before graduation.

At length, the great day dawned for Rebecca—a day to which she had been looking forward for five years. Silently she stole out of bed, crept to the window, and threw open the blinds to welcome the cloudless morning. Even the sun looked different, somehow—larger, redder, more important than usual.

"It's going to be a beautiful day," Emma Jane said from her bed. "Did you sleep well?"

"Not really. I'm too excited," Rebecca replied.

Even the Sun Looked Different.

"We better hurry and get dressed or we'll be late for the ceremony."

Wareham was its very busiest ever on this day of days. Parents and relatives of students had been arriving on the train and driving into town all morning. Former pupils, both married and single, streamed back into the dear old village.

The two livery stables were crowded with vehicles of all sorts, and lines of buggies and wagons were drawn up along the sides of the shady roads, the horses switching their tails in luxurious idleness. The streets swarmed with people wearing their fanciest clothes.

Adam Ladd, who had just arrived from Portland, stood under a tree near the Wareham school church waiting to see the graduates march by. Instead, the twelve girls and ten boys of the senior class rode through the streets on a haycart decked with green vines and bunches of long-stemmed field daisies. Rebecca, the class president, drove the vehicle.

Under a Tree, Waiting

She was seated on a green covered bench that looked very much like a throne. As the June sunlight filtered down on her hair, she looked truly beautiful.

The interior of the church was hot, and the air was still and breathless. The essays, songs, and recitations began as soon as the graduates were seated. When Rebecca read the class poem, "Makers of Tomorrow", which she had written herself, she received a thunderous ovation.

In the audience, Rebecca spotted Hannah and Will and her brother John and Cousin Ann. She missed her mother's smiling face, but knew she couldn't leave the farm or the children to come to Wareham. She spied Mr. and Mrs. Cobb in the crowd, as well as many other Riverboro folks, but didn't see her Aunt Jane. She knew Aunt Miranda couldn't attend, but where on this special occasion was her beloved Aunt Jane?

Suddenly, it was time for the presentation of

She Received a Thunderous Ovation.

the diplomas. As each graduate came forward to shake hands with Mr. Morrison, the principal, and receive that cherished diploma, the audience applauded enthusiastically.

When it was over, and the crowd had thinned out a bit, Adam Ladd made his way to the platform.

Rebecca turned from speaking to some strangers and met him in the aisle. "Oh, Mr. Aladdin, I'm so glad you could come! Tell me," the seventeen year old girl said shyly, "were you pleased with my record here at the Academy?"

"More than pleased," he said. "I'm glad I met the child, proud I know the girl, longing to meet the woman!"

Rebecca's heart skipped a beat at this sweet praise. Before she could find the words to thank him, Mr. and Mrs. Cobb approached her, and she introduced them to Mr. Ladd.

"Where is Aunt Jane?" Rebecca cried, holding Mrs. Cobb's hand on one side and Mr.

Adam Ladd Made His Way to the Platform.

Cobb's on the other.

"I'm sorry, lovey, but we've got bad news for you," Mrs. Cobb said gently.

"Is Aunt Miranda worse? She is. I can tell just by looking at you." All the color drained from Rebecca's face.

"She had a stroke yesterday morning when she was helping Jane lay out her clothes to come here today. Jane made us promise not to tell you until graduation exercises were over."

"Poor Aunt Miranda!" cried a shocked Rebecca. "I must go home right away. But I have so much to do before I can leave."

"I'll pack your trunk for you, Becky," offered Emma Jane, who had rushed over as soon as she heard the sad news. "Don't worry about a thing. You'll be able to leave tomorrow."

After Rebecca and Emma Jane hurried off to their dormitory, Mr. Ladd crossed the common and ran into Emily Maxwell. Immediately, he told her the bad news from Riverboro.

"What a tragedy!" Miss Maxwell exclaimed.

"We've Got Bad News for You."

"I had so many plans for Rebecca, and now she'll have to settle down to nurse that poor, sick, cross, old aunt."

"If it hadn't been for that cross old aunt, Rebecca would never have come to Wareham," Mr. Ladd reminded his colleague.

"That's true," Miss Maxwell admitted. "It's just that I thought a happier day was dawning for Rebecca."

"It is, I assure you. The railroad is going to buy the right of way through Mrs. Randall's land for six thousand dollars," he explained. "That will yield the good lady about four hundred dollars a year if she will let me invest her money. She ought to be able to pay off the mortgage after that. With Rebecca working, life will definitely improve for that family."

"I confess I want Rebecca to have a career," Miss Maxwell said.

"I don't," Mr. Ladd retorted. "You understand her mind but not necessarily her heart. I think it's important she follows her heart."

"I Had So Many Plans for Rebecca."

"Yes, particularly if her heart beckons your way," said Miss Maxwell, looking at him with a knowing smile.

"If Her Heart Beckons Your Way."

She Asked for Her Niece.

Chapter Fourteen

The Dawning of a New Day

The day after graduation at Wareham Academy, Rebecca took the train to Riverboro. She did not see her Aunt Miranda till she had been at the brick house for several days.

Then one morning when Miranda was feeling better, she asked for her niece. The door opened into the dim sick room, and Rebecca stood there with the sunlight behind her, her hands full of beautiful bachelor buttons.

Miranda's pale, sharp face looked haggard on the pillow, and her body appeared thin under the blanket.

"Come in," her aunt ordered. "I'm not dead yet. Don't mess up the bed with those flowers."

"Oh, no! They're going in a glass pitcher," said Rebecca, turning to the washstand. She tried desperately to control her voice and stop the tears that sprang to her eyes.

"Let me look at you; come closer. What dress are you wearing?" her aunt asked in a cracked weak voice.

"My blue calico," Rebecca answered.

"Are you taking good care of your green cashmere?" her aunt wanted to know.

"Yes, Aunt Miranda."

"What bones has your brother Mark broken since I've been sick?"

"None at all, Aunt Miranda."

"How's John turning out?" Miranda inquired.

"He's going to be the best one of us all," Rebecca replied.

"I hope you're doing things right in the kitchen." Miranda sighed. "Do you scald the

"I'm Not Dead Yet."

coffee pot and turn it upside down on the window sill?"

"Yes, Aunt Miranda."

"It's always 'yes' with you and 'yes' with Jane," groaned Miranda, trying to move her stiffened body, "but all the time I lay here knowing things aren't being done the way I like them."

There was a long pause, during which time Rebecca sat down on the bed and timidly touched her aunt's hand. Looking at her gaunt face and closed eyes, Rebecca felt tremendous compassion for her.

"Aunt Miranda, I want you to know I'm all grown up and graduated—number three in a class of twenty-two. I've had two good positions offered me already. If you want me near, I'll take the Edgewood School, so that I can be here nights and Sundays to help. If you get better, I'll take the job in Augusta because it pays a hundred dollars more."

"You listen to me," said Miranda, her voice

She Touched Her Aunt's Hand.

quaking. "You take the best job, regardless of me. I'd like to live long enough to know if you'd paid off that mortgage, but I guess I won't."

Here Miranda stopped talking, and Rebecca stole out of the room to cry by herself. Yet as the days passed, Miranda grew stronger and stronger. Finally, she was able to sit in the chair by the window. Hope began to steal back into Rebecca's heart.

Then one day, a telegram came from Hannah: "Come at once. Mother has had a bad accident."

In less than one hour, Rebecca was on her way to Sunnybrook Farm, terribly frightened as to what might be awaiting her at her journey's end.

Aurelia Randall had been standing on the haymow in the barn when she had a dizzy spell and suffered a bad fall. Her right knee was fractured and her back strained and sore. It was obvious that she would require complete bed rest for a long time.

A Telegram from Hannah

During the next two months, Rebecca devoted herself to cooking, washing, ironing, mending, chasing after the three younger children, and caring for an invalid mother. No seventeen year old girl could pass through such an ordeal and come out unchanged. Yet as hard a time as it was, it forged a close bond between mother and daughter.

One afternoon as Mrs. Randall and Rebecca sat chatting on the front porch, Will Melville drove by and tossed a letter into Rebecca's lap.

"Sister's not worse, then," said Aurelia Randall gratefully, "or Jane would have telegraphed. See what she has to say."

Rebecca opened the envelope and read in one flash of an eye the whole brief page:

"Your Aunt Miranda passed away an hour ago. Come at once, if your mother is out of danger. I shall not have the funeral till you are here. She died very suddenly and without pain. Oh, Rebecca! I miss you!

Aunt Jane"

A Letter into Rebecca's Lap

"Poor Aunt Miranda," cried Rebecca, bursting into tears. "She didn't have a very happy life, I'm afraid. Oh, I feel terrible that I didn't get to tell her good-bye. And now, Aunt Jane is all alone, and I am torn between going to her and staying with you."

"You must go to Riverboro this very instant," said Mrs. Randall, sitting up from her pillows. "Your aunts have done everything in the world for you. Now it is your turn to show your gratitude. Anyhow the doctor says I've turned the corner."

"But, mother, I can't go!" Rebecca lamented. "Who'll take care of you?"

"Hannah can help out for a while," Mrs. Randall answered quickly. "Now you go pack your bag. Oh, how I wish I could go to my sister's funeral and prove that I've forgiven her for the unkind things she said when Lorenzo and I got married."

"Why do you think she behaved so badly?" Rebecca probed curiously, remembering only

"You Must Go."

too well her Aunt Miranda's hostile attitude toward her father.

"Once when we were all young and single, your father asked me to lead the grand march with him at the Christmas ball in Riverboro. I found out afterward that Miranda thought he intended to ask her. I don't think she ever got over that terrible hurt."

At this point, Aurelia Randall broke down and wept bitterly, and Rebecca put her arms around her mother to comfort her. Then she gave her a kiss and slipped upstairs to pack.

Later that day, when Will drove Rebecca to Temperance to catch the train, they saw the first railroad surveyors at work on the property. Rebecca caught her breath. "The time has come," she thought sadly. "When I leave here today, I'm saying good-bye to Sunnybrook Farm."

It was a great comfort to Rebecca to see Jeremiah Cobb waiting for her at the stage when she arrived in Maplewood. "Oh, Mr. Cobb," she

Surveyors at Work

sobbed, flinging herself on his shoulder. "So much has happened since I made my first trip to Riverboro with you so long ago. Oh, I do dread going to the brick house now that Aunt Miranda is gone."

"There, there, lovey," her old friend whispered comfortingly, "we'll be all alone on the stage, and we'll talk things over. You'll feel better by the time we get there."

When they finally saw the chimneys of Riverboro, Rebecca asked Mr. Cobb just to drop her in front of the brick house. Hearing the rumble of the stage, Jane Sawyer, frail and trembling, rushed out to greet her niece. Rebecca held out her arms, and the two women embraced tenderly.

"Rebecca, do you feel any bitterness over anything Miranda ever said to you?" her Aunt Jane asked.

"No, I've come here with a heart full of gratitude," Rebecca said, her voice choking.

"Miranda was a good person, Rebecca," her

"A Heart Full of Gratitude"

aunt continued, "but she had a sharp tongue. She never said so, but I'm sure she was sorry for some of the unkind things she said to you. In the end, she did something to show you how she really felt about you. She willed the brick house and all the land to you."

"Oh, I'd give anything to thank her," Rebecca said, overwhelmed by deep emotion. "I think I will go inside and be alone with her for a while."

Later Rebecca came back outside and sat on the front steps of the brick house and listened to the call of the river as it dashed to the sea. This was all her home now—her roof, her garden, her green acres, her stately trees. It would be shelter for the children at Sunnybrook Farm and a haven for her dear mother.

Rebecca's own future was uncertain. It was still hidden in beautiful mists. Only time would tell whether she would be a remarkable teacher or a great writer, but she knew for sure that happiness lay ahead.